SILLY BILLY!

SILLY BILLY!

BY **Pat Hutchins**

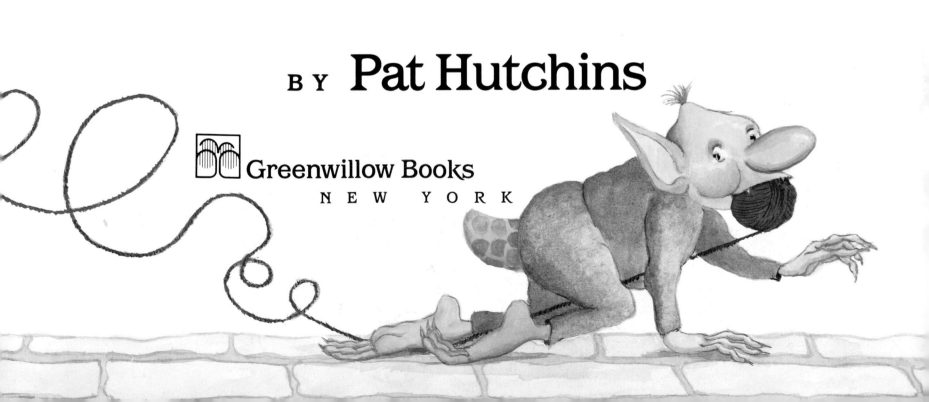 **Greenwillow Books**
N E W Y O R K

Watercolor paints and pen and ink
were used for the full-color art.
The text type is ITC Barcelona Medium.

Printed in Hong Kong by
South China Printing Company (1988) Ltd.
First Edition
1 2 3 4 5 6 7 8 9 10

Library of Congress Cataloging-in-Publication Data
Hutchins, Pat (date)
Silly Billy! / by Pat Hutchins.
p.   cm.
Summary: Little brother Billy ruins
all his sister's attempts to play
and is excused by the grownups
because he's "only little."
ISBN 0-688-10817-2.
ISBN 0-688-10818-0 (lib. bdg.)
(1. Brothers and sisters—Fiction.
2. Monsters—Fiction.)
I. Title.
PZ7.H96165Sh   1992
(E)—dc20
91-32561   CIP   AC

FOR SUSAN **HIRSCHMAN**!

Hazel was playing a game with Grandpa,
Grandma, and Ma and Pa.
Billy wanted to play, too.

"Let Billy have a turn," said Grandma.

"He's only little."

Billy tossed the board up and threw the cards into the air.

"SILLY BILLY!" said Hazel. "You've spoiled my game. I might as well play with my dollhouse."

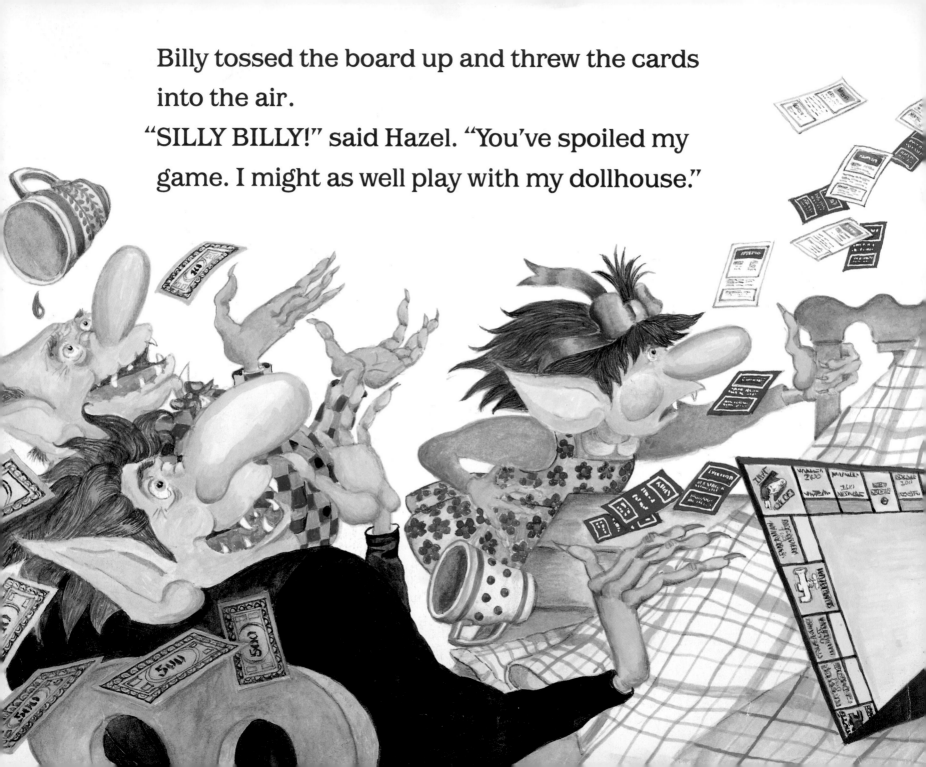

But Billy wanted to play with the dollhouse, too.

"Let Billy have a turn," said Grandpa.

"He's only little."

Billy tipped the dollhouse on its side,
and all the furniture fell out.

"SILLY BILLY!" said Hazel. "You've spoiled my game.
I might as well play with the building blocks."

But Billy wanted to play
with the building blocks, too.

"Let Billy have a turn," said Ma.
"He's only little."

Billy knocked all the bricks
down and jumbled them up.
"SILLY BILLY!" said Hazel.
"You've spoiled my game.
I might as well play with the train set."

But Billy wanted to play
with the train set, too.

"Let Billy have a turn," said Pa.
"He's only little."

Billy pulled the tracks to bits
and unhooked the wagons.
"SILLY BILLY!" said Hazel.
"You've spoiled all my games.
I might as well go to sleep in the toy box!"

But Billy wanted to sleep in the toy box, too.

"Let Billy have a turn," said Ma and Pa
   and Grandma and Grandpa.
"He's only little."

So Billy went to sleep in the toy box.

And Hazel put the train set back together,

and built the bricks up again,

and turned the dollhouse the right way up.

"Silly Billy," said Hazel.

Since the publication of *Rosie's Walk* in 1968, reviewers on both sides of the Atlantic have been loud in their praise of Pat Hutchins's work. Among her popular picture books are *Tidy Titch*; *What Game Shall We Play?*; *Where's the Baby?* (an *SLJ* Best Book of the Year); *The Doorbell Rang* (an ALA Notable Book); *You'll Soon Grow into Them, Titch*; and *The Wind Blew* (winner of the 1974 Kate Greenaway Medal). For older readers she has written several novels, including *The House That Sailed Away*, *The Curse of the Egyptian Mummy*, and *Rats!* Pat Hutchins, her husband, Laurence, and their sons, Morgan and Sam, live in London, England.